Desiree Fern

Zachary Duresky

authorHOUSE®

AuthorHouse™
1663 Liberty Drive
Bloomington, IN 47403
www.authorhouse.com
Phone: 1-800-839-8640

Published by AuthorHouse 10/09/2014

ISBN: 978-1-4969-4583-9 (sc)
ISBN: 978-1-4969-4584-6 (e)

Library of Congress Control Number: 2014918170

Contents

Part 1

Puritanism. What an idiotic word. Dost thou think so? It's so stupid. It means fearing God, restricting one's life, and preventing oneself from any pleasurable experiences. My home, some village in Virginia, is crawling with Puritanism. Everyone fears God, restricts their lives, and prevents themselves from any pleasurable experiences. I may live amongst puritans, but a puritan, I am not!

My name is Desiree. Desiree Fern. I love that name. So beautiful and elegant, to match myself. I don't show modesty for my beauty. With my long, waving brown hair, my seductive eyes of the same color, my lips of pale red, my bosom of a large and pouting size, and my overall curved and sensual figure, I am proud to say that I am beautiful.

I do not agree with the restricted, paranoid, and boring ways of my village. I do whatever I want, regardless of what the villagers that surround me think. Them saying I will burn in Hell, I am a disgrace to the Lord, I am a possible witch. But society is foolish and stupid (in addition to being boring). I love to have fun, and enjoy all of the pleasure that there are, and not worry about religion. I do not make religion what I was born for. That's not a life to me. To put more passion into what I feel, I wrote a song about it. I love to write songs. It's one of my many pleasures that I allow myself to enjoy unflinchingly.

Sin Fulfilled Life

I forget what the preacher says,

what the village is forced to believe,

it's a hellish life for them all,

makes one feel like they want to leave.

Leave this town,

or leave this life,

3

leave and be dead,

pull out the knife.

What's the point in living,

when living in fear?

Fear of the Lord,

always holding a tear.

That's not the life for me,

I'd kill myself before I live it.

I'd never take it from my people,

and especially never give it.

I live my life to its full,

I skip the boring church,

don't do any praying,

skipping those never hurts.

I enjoy the beauty of the woods,

eat as much delicious food as I can,

invent games to play all day,

and make love to a handsome man.

Sin fulfilled life,

that's what I carry,

everyone says I'm evil,

well I'm no Virgin Mary.

Sin fulfilled life,

that's what I carry,

everyone says I'm evil,

well I'm no Virgin Mary.

Sin fulfilled life,

that's what I carry,

everyone says I'm evil,

well I'm no Virgin Mary.

It's now two days before my sixteenth birthday. It's Sunday, so naturally everyone's at church. Except for me of course. I prefer to spend my Sunday afternoon swimming in the James River. I like to dive into the deepest part of it, climb onto the rocks, swim with the rushing current, and see all of the fish. It is a tremendous pleasure. But dost thou know what is even more pleasurable? That would be making love. I usually lose track of the time as I swim on Sundays; but today, I had my eye on a very handsome boy who was attending church. His name was Arthur Monroe. He was a virgin, unlike the married men in the village, or the ones I've already made love to. Well, that was all going to change. I was in need of a strong, handsome man beside me; one I've not been with yet; one to bring me so much surging pleasure. So, I made sure I kept track of the time for when church was over, and left for the village at the right moment. Time estimation, it's an important skill.

I made it back, and watched all of the people exit the church in their usual ways. The men looking straight on with cold, stern faces, the women with their heads bowed and their hands clapped together, looking so miserable. All wearing their usual attire. The men, with their scary black hats and bland clothing. The women, with their pure white aprons, tight hoods hiding their hair, and heavily covered in clothing that hides nearly everything but their face. I had my usual attire on as well. A short, revealing dress made of purplish-red silk. I made it myself since no designer here would dare make a dress like mine. My legs, my mid-drift, and my cleavage all easily noticeable; it's kind of a way to tease the men around here. To make them want to see more. And of course, I have nothing to hide my lovely hair. It flows freely, just like me.

There was Arthur Monroe, exiting the church along with everyone else, looking just as cold as the other men. Just like me, he wasn't married yet, so I saw nothing wrong with making love to him. I would not be committing adultery, so no Commandments would be broken. I make sure of that with every man I sleep with. I strolled up to him within the crowd, everyone looking at me with disgust and disapproval, as usual.

"Hello Arthur," I said casually.

"Hello Desiree," he responded. I continued walking with him, as if I were just going in the same direction as he. But I continued to turn my eyes to him with a subtle smirk.

"Dost thou want something Desiree?" he asked.

"I was wondering if thee would like to come to my house for an hour or two. My father's helping the preacher educate his apprentice." What I was saying was true. My father, Jonathan Fern, really was helping educate the new apprentice, a young man named Edward Hawthorne. That made this the perfect time to bring a man over. Father's suspicions would not be aroused. But I was about to arouse something else.

It took me some persuasion, but I managed to bring Arthur to my house. He thought I just wanted casual company. Naivety, so charming.

"So," he began as we walked in, "dost thou want to pray for forgiveness?"

"Forgiveness? For what?"

"For skipping church, again. And for thy numerous other sins. I could pray with thee, a group prayer is always nice."

"Maybe. But first, wouldst thou like to hear my new song?"

"Um, alright."

"Just sit down on the chair over there and get comfortable."

"Alright." After he sat down, I walked up to him, and sat on my knees, looking at him with lustful hunger in my eyes. Beads of sweat emerged from his forehead. He began to suspect what was truly happening.

Hold on to Me

Thou was looking so miserable,

that thee was,

Out of that church thee walked.

So long thee hath been repressing,

Repressing thou urges,

a lifelong battle thee fought.

Well, thee can end the war,

end it here right now,

set thou withdrawn emotions free.

Because I'm here for thee,

thee and only thee,

let loose thou feelings on me.

I want thee to hold me close,

Hold me tighter and tighter,

I want my excitement to scream.

Only thee can do that,

I know thee can,

make being awake feel like a dream.

So much repression,

thou hath been holding on,

but I want thee to hold on to me.

So much repression,

thou hath been holding on,

but I want thee to hold on to me.

So much repression,

thou hath been holding on,

but I want thee to hold on to me.

Once I sung the last lyric, I leapt on to him. We both thudded onto the floor, but I didn't care, I was so lust driven by the time my song was over. I had him down on the floor with my arms around him, and I began to smear my lips all over his face. I kissed him mercilessly and held on with all of my might, making sure he could not get away. He struggled at first, but very quickly he stopped, and succumbed to my advances. And we made it.

An hour later, we finally finished (even though I could've gone on for much longer). I was sure that Arthur had enough for his first time, so I had us end it. I finally stopped kissing him and had my inescapable arms let go. I started to get up, but he was still lying on the floor. He was worn out but obviously satisfied. I pulled out my special pocket sized mirror I made myself from out of the breast pocket in my dress. I looked in to it and began to fix my hair.

"Thou best be getting back to thy home, Arthur," I said. "Not much else to do."

"Y…Y…Yes, my heavenly, b…b….being," he rasped from his panting mouth.

"Such kind words," I responded with a chuckle. Arthur stood up on his feet, put his pants back on, then exited out of the back door.

After Arthur left, I picked the chair back up and spent the next few moments sitting in it and fixing my hair some more. Then, father stormed in unexpectedly. He slammed the door and glared at me with rage.

"Why art thou home so early father?" I asked innocently, "Thee was not supposed to be back for another hour."

"Young Edward shows much promise; he dost not need much teaching. So, we ended early. And when I got here, I saw a young man step out of the back door. Didst thou lay thy filthy sin upon him, as thou dost to every man thee comes across?"

"Of course I did."

"That's just it? Thou hath committed yet another unholy deed, and thou feels no shame nor pleads forgiveness?" he shouted with so much anger.

"Correct father," I said in my usual calm tone. Then I stuck my mirror back in my bosom pocket.

"Thou rat-eating tramp!" my father shouted, "this be the final straw! Thou will learn how to be Christian, or die at my hands!"

"Father," I said firmly, 'Thou art just as head-beaten as all others here. God did not create us so we could fear him." At that, he struck me across the left cheek with the back of his left hand. I was sent thundering to the floor with a heavy thud. The floor hurt, but my cheek stung like it was touched by a blacksmith tool with a burning tip. Then I tried to get back up, but father stomped his foot on my back, holding it there, pressing me to the floor.

"TRAMP!" he screamed like a preacher during a sermon, "WE WERER CREATED TO FEAR THE FATHER! THE HOLY FATHER AND THE FATHER OF THE HOUSE! I'M THE FATHER OF THE HOUSE! YOU <u>WILL</u> LEARN TO FEAR GOD, AND ME!" His foot pressed harder, heavily squeezing the air out of me. "THOU WILLST GO TO HELL, BURN WITH UNENDING FLAMES, SATAN TORMENTING THEE FOR ALL ETERNITY, UNLES YOU SUCCUMB TO THY TWO FATHERS!" I glared up at father defiantly. I knew I had done nothing to deserve Satan's fire. Arthur Monroe may have succumbed to me, but I was stronger. I was not going to succumb to father's words, no matter how loud he was, or how much I could not breathe.

"No father," I rasped, "Thou words are lies. Lies from Hell!" Then, father used his other foot to give me a hard kick in my left side. I squealed in pain. Then father finally took his foot off of me, and I rolled on to my right side, clutching my left side in pain with tears rolling down my cheeks. Father gazed down at me, with no sympathy in his hateful eyes.

"Thou hath better start praying for thy only soul, because I won't do it for thee." He then went and sat at the dinner table. I struggled back to my feet and went to cook our dinner.

The next day, father sent me out to by some food at the market. When I got there, I encountered my best friend, Emily Carter.

"Hello Emily," I said with excitement.

"Hello Desiree. Art thou shopping as well?"

"Yes, for my father and myself."

"If thou had a husband, you could shop for him, just as I do for mine. Shop for him instead of thy father."

"Well, what am I supposed to do? No man wants to marry me."

"It's because of thou blasphemy-filled behavior. Every man is afraid to marry thee. My husband is not even happy that I am friends with thee."

"I still see nothing wrong with my behavior."

"But the Holy Father dost not want thou to be that way. Hell is waiting for thee Desiree." All I could do was laugh at that. "Please Desiree," Emily went on anxiously, "listen to me. I'm thou best friend. I don't want thou to suffer for all eternity."

"I will not suffer Emily, please do not worry about that," I said as I held on to her hands.

"Well, whilst thou at least turn your life around?" Emily asked, "Everyone in this town hates thee because of thou heathen acts. The way thee dresses, the sermons thee skips, the lack of Bible reading, and the seduction of pure men."

"Oh, like Arthur Monroe?"

"What? Another one? Now there art too many to count. Desiree, thou must stop this."

"All of the men I seduce are not married; therefore I'm doing no harm."

"Yes thou art. Thou art sending them to damnation."

"Damnation, damnation, damnation!" I chanted in a mocking tone, "Is that all everyone thinks about?"

"Thou hast heard what the sermons say."

"Well, the sermons are not God, and I refuse to believe that God hates us so much that he sends us to Hell for the smallest sin."

"I'm just scarred for thee, Desiree."

"And I'm worried about thee Emily. These teachings and the thinking of all around us hath taken the woman out of thee."

"What?"

"Thou art afraid of your beauty." As I said that, I pulled out my mirror and showed it to her. "Look at thou reflection. Thou art beautiful Emily." She truly was. She had lovely blue eyes, thin yellow eyebrows, a small, precious nose, full pink lips, and velvety skin. I could not see her hair, since she had it covered, just like the other women. But I've seen it before, and it's beautiful yellow hair. "Thou art a very beautiful woman, and thanks to these teachings, thou art afraid to flaunt it and be proud of it. Thou tries to hide it, like all other women; you're afraid to show the world that you're a woman."

"I wish I weren't beautiful," she said as she turned away from the mirror in fear. "My beauty might entice a man someday, and if it does it's my fault."

"'Oh I give up," I said with a chuckle, "Thou art hopeless," I said as I gave her a playful hug. Emily actually managed to laugh and hug back. That made me feel so happy.

Emily and I did our shopping together. Once we started, I bought a branch filled with grapes to eat for myself as we shopped. They were red grapes, my favorite. They were delicious; not even slightly sour, and so sweet and juicy. And then my eyes caught something that really brought water to my mouth. It was Edward Hawthorne, the preacher's apprentice. He was exceedingly handsome. He was five feet, ten inches tall; exceeding my height by six inches (a girl always finds a man taller than her very arousing). He had short brown hair, dark green eyes, and a broad chin and shoulders. He was so handsome. I had to give him my passion and fire.

"I will see thee again momentarily Emily," I said, not taking my focused eyes off of Edward. "A new embrace is calling for me." Emily turned her attention to where my eyes were looking.

"Edward Hawthorne? Oh no Desiree. Thou shalt not send the Devil on our new preacher to be."

"I don't know what thou said; all I can hear is his hunger calling me." I started to approach him, leaving Emily behind.

"Desiree, please do not." I ignored her and went onward. When I feel lust in my soul, it's all I dedicate to.

"Excuse me, Mr. Hawthorne," I said as I made it up to him, continuing to eat my grapes and carrying my full food basket.

"Good day, Desiree Fern," he said to me, trying to sound powerful and wise (just because the preacher and my father love him).

"Whilst thou like the last of my grapes?" I asked in ladies fashion.

"That is kind of thee, but no thanks. Is that all?"

"No, I have something important to ask, but it's crowded here in the market. Can we talk in the woods?"

"Young lady, I know of what thou does to men. I do not trust thee alone with me.

"It's very important, please."

"Well alright. But thee must swear to our Lord, that thee will not…"

"Hurry!" I interrupted as I threw away my grape branch and used my now free hand to grab his and pull him along with me into the woods. I had to interrupt him; I never make promises that I won't keep.

"All right Desiree," Edward said with exhaust in his breath, "We're in the woods. Now what is it that is so important?"

"I have a song that I want thee to hear."

"That's what thee dragged me into the woods for, a song?"

"I want the soon to be great preacher to approve of it?" I said as innocently as I could.

"What I do not approve of is thou deeds of damnation that all in this village knows about. Thy father told me about how he had to raise you alone after thy mother died in childbirth. And thou sinfulness shows much ungratefulness." He thought he sounded so old and wise, when in reality; he was only two years above my age. "Thou art lucky to still have one birth parent. My mother died in childbirth as well, and then my father killed himself. If it were not for the preacher taking me in and raising me as his very own child, I would not be here today. I show gratitude toward him every day, and I think thee ought to do the same for thy one and only birth parent."

"I am grateful to my father. Despite his daily abusive acts, I feel deep love for him. That's why I go through the trouble to buy our food and do the cooking for him."

"That is not very much gratitude, I'm sorry to say."

"Well, maybe I can learn to be better. I want to start with pleasing you better since thou art our preacher to be."

"Start with me?"

"Yes, I'm so used to my sinful and devilish acts that I need to slowly work at changing. Maybe thee can help with my fist steps."

"That sounds divine. Maybe God hath finally come into thy life. How can I help?"

"Well, maybe thee could start by approving of my song. It's a Lord praising song that I wrote myself."

"A wonderful way to start. Let me hear it." I never promised that it was a Lord praising song.

My Lust Has No Control

Alone with thee is what I want,

and what thee wants with me, I know,

thee knows I'm irresistible,

and thee doesn't want me to go.

Never been together before,

we've always been away,

but now we're alone and free,

let's make our time worth to stay.

Thou hath been so repressed,

raised from within the gloom,

but I have come to free thee,

take thee out of that room.

My lust has no control,

I want to give it all,

to thee.

Make thee a real man,

the best one there could,

ever be.

My lust has no control,

I want to give it all,

to thee.

Make thee a real man,

the best one there could,

ever be.

All thou has to do is kiss,

kiss me until I'm lifted,

and I shall kiss thee right back,

for kissing, I'm so gifted.

I want thee to spread thy arms,

then grab on and hold me,

and as we go at it,

maybe thou could scold me.

My lust has no control,

I want to give it all,

to thee.

Make thee a real man,

the best one there could,

ever be.

My lust has no control,

I want to give it all,

to thee.

Make thee a real man,

the best one there could,

ever be.

"That's no Lord praising song!" Edward said enraged, "That be a Devil's song!"

"It is not. The Devil cannot make my beauty," I said as I put my left hand on my left hip in a provocative way.

"How dare thee defy me?" I then walked up closer to him, we were nearly face to face.

"Like this," I said as I waved my right hand in front of his face while wiggling my fingers. He looked at my hand with deep confusion. Perfect, he was distracted. "And like this," I said as I grabbed his groin with my left hand. There was a look of sudden surprise on his delicious face. I could feel movement down there, I knew he liked it. "I take it thou hath never felt that before," I said teasingly.

"I... I feel nothing."

"Liar. But just in case..." then I grabbed the stubborn denial wielder, and pressed my lips hard against his. Now there was intense movement down there. I then pulled him down to the ground with me. He struggled at first like Arthur did (most men do), then he just lay still on the ground and allowed my lips to smother every part of his face. I had him now. Then I worked both hands this time to his groin, and tried to pull off his pants. Suddenly, he started struggling again.

"NO, NO!" he yelped. But I continued trying to get his pants off, while my savory lips kept doing their job. "STOP IT!" he shouted, the he suddenly pushed me off aggressively. I ended up rolling on to my back, feeling all of the leaves, sticks and dirt. I turned my head to the right and saw him getting back to his feet and pulling his pants all of the way up.

"Dost thou really think we can just stop now?" I said as I crawled back up, "I was merely getting started." I could feel myself burning inside, and he was burning all over, I was not about to let him leave now.

"Leave me be tramp!" he said filled with anger, "What thou hath done was un-Godly!"

"But thou liked it, you cannot hide that from me," I said as I walked up to him again. He turned his back to walk away. "Come back here my love," I said as I wrapped my arms around his powerful chest, and began to kiss the left side of his neck. He quickly broke free of my grasp and my lips with a loud grunt, and swiftly spun around to swing his left fist at my left cheek, thundering me to the ground. My face was in the dirt, and the pain was excruciating. Not even father hit me that hard. I pulled my face out the dirt, I had tears in my eyes, but I was too angry to start crying. I looked up at this blazingly damned, unbearable beast with my teary eyes scorching like Hellfire.

"Thou hath made me do that," the arrogant lair said to me in a fake calm voice.

"That I did not! Thee has self-control!" I shouted though gritted teeth.

"Thou hath done wrong, but I forgive thee, as a true Christian does."

"Forgive me? I've done nothing wrong! Thou hath lost your self-control and showed wrath, one of the seven the deadly sins! Thou art not so perfect, thou hath committed a sin!"

"SHUT UP WHORE! I'm going back to the church, the preachers expecting me. Just stay away from me from now on."

"With pleasure, thou woman hitting BASTARD!" I shouted with as much rage that I could muster. His teeth gritted very tightly as he looked at me, they looked as if they were about to break. His fist rose again. But then he shut his eyes, clearly trying to calm down then he lowered his arm and walked away. That bastard showed no Christianity today. He hurt my cheek agonizingly. He had no deserving of my lust. So, I decided to put him out of my thoughts, and went to pick up my food basket that I left under a nearby tree, and then I went home.

"WHER HATH THOU BEEN?" demanded father when he saw how filthy I was and the red mark on my cheek.

"With a man of course, but I still got the food," I said holding up the market basket.

"PUT IT ON THE TABLE AND EXPLAIN THY SELF!" I did as he said and put the basket on the table. "Who was it this time?"

"Edward Hawthorne. But nothing happened."

"HAWTHORNE? THEE DARES TO WASH AWAY THAT YOUNG MANS PURITY? OUR SOON TO BE PREACHER?"

"Nothing happened I said. He shook out of my embrace, and then he gave me this here mark."

"Thee deserves it. He did right. But he must forgive thee."

"FORGIVE ME?" THOU ART JUST AS STUPID AS THAT HORRIBLE BASTARD!"

"WHAT?"

"AS STUPID AS ALL OF THE OTHER MINDLESS SWINE THAT MAKE UP OUR VILLAGE!"

"THEE DARES TO TALK TO ME LIKE THAT?" he said coming up to me in a threatening manner.

"Thou hath never frightened me before father. And thou dose not today." I meant what I said, father has never scarred me. And after what Hawthorne did to me, I was in no mood for father to beat me today (or ever again). I channeled my anger against Hawthorne to father.

"THOU SIN-LOVING SLUT!" he thundered as he raised his arm to hit me as usual. And as it came down I grabbed his wrist, stopping him. Father looked surprised, I've never done this before.

"Thou shalt hit me no more father. I am a woman, and will be even more of one tomorrow on my sixteenth birthday. Things shall be different around her from now on." Father's confusion turned to anger, and he raised his other arm to grab my neck. But I stopped that one two.

"BITCH!" he shouted.

"Oh, watch the cursing father, our good Lord does not like that." He pulled back both of his hands angrily, his eyes now burning with fiery intensity.

"I WILL KILL THEE!" he shouted.

"Dost thou truly want to do such a thing?" I said, having more fun mocking him. "Break one of the Ten Commandments; meet Satan in the afterlife; defy all that thou preaches? Well go ahead. Put me out of my misery, show the sin thee is capable of. Like thou always does." I said with challenge in my voice and my eyes. I stood there waiting for him to do something. He had his hands up, looking as if they were strangling something invisible. And just as I predicted, he did not advance. He just gritted his teeth tightly, his forehead sprouting a vain, and red flushing his face. And then he put his hands down with a frustrated grunt, and looked down at the floor. "That's better father," I said as I walked up and kissed him on the left cheek. "Now I will make our dinner."

I was so proud of myself. I finally stood up to father. Showed him that I ran my own life. Showed that no one, not the preacher, not Edward Hawthorne, and especially he, has any control over me. I could tell that my life was inevitably, going to change.

Part 2

My birthday, the very next morning. I woke up from a peaceful sleep, ready to unleash my energy on the day. I began by stretching out my arms above my head, letting them loosen up. But then all of the sudden, a flash burst out of the finger tips on my left hand. I yelped and threw myself back against the bed, keeping my left hand in the air. The flash was gone now. But what was it? I still kept my hand up, and this time I tried to see if I could make whatever happened happen again. I thought hard, stretched my arm out as far as I could, and then the lights came out again. Then I pulled them back in by not stretching as much and letting loose my concentration. Then I stretched and concentrated again, and they came out. This time I brought my arm down gradually and looked at them. As I examined them, I saw that they were five mystical claws made of a sort of blinding white light. Each one sticking out of one finger tip. What were these glowing claws? I decided to test them. So, I brought my hand underneath the bed, and touched the floor with them. The claws went right through it. The floor under my bed was now left with five gaping holes. Nervously, I pulled the claws back in. Then I looked at the candle on my nightstand. I extend the claws again, and ever so slightly touched it with the claw on the finger next to my thumb. The candle instantly broke in half. I was getting worried; I had to know exactly how powerful these claws were. So I snuck out of the house through my window, being careful not to let the claws come out and cut through the house. I snuck to the James River. There were all of these enormous boulders and rocks surrounding the river, very hard for even the strongest man to break (a perfect test). So, I extended my claws again, went over to one of the biggest rocks, and gently touched my claws to it. Just as I touched it, the rock crumbled to pieces. The pieces fell into the river and got swept away. These claws were dangerous. I did not know how, or why I got them, I just knew I had to learn how to control them.

For the next week, I spent my free time teaching myself how to control my mystical claws. I was staying away from close contact with people until I was sure I knew how to control them. That meant keeping an even bigger distance between father and me, not seeing Emily, and not making love to any men. As the week neared to an end, I was finally managing it. I could make the claws come out and go back in at will. They were only coming out when I commanded them. Now that I had my new found power under control, I developed a fondness for it. I found my claws to be beautiful and fascinating. They were lethal, but I knew how to keep them under control. It still not even being a week since I discovered my power, but now that I had it under control, I now spent my free time just sitting in my room and looking at them; admiring their beauty and awe. They even became the inspiration for my next song.

<u>Everything Amazing</u>

I bring with me something no one else can have.

A thrill to hold and bring energy to the sky.

Just inside my fingers I carry what can cut in half.

Fills me with the feeling of being able to fly.

At my command with just the will of my thought.

A power of gods with death at a single strike.

Can handle any struggle and battle that is brought.

Can glow and shine to be seen in the darkest night.

I can bring the light,

I can summon with all of my will.

My amazing gift,

it brings all of the shine.

Everything amazing,

I can claim as mine.

Everything amazing,

I can claim as mine.

Everyone wants a life like mine, that's what they truly want.

Live with a spirit that's free and a power that beams.

No one can ever know what it's like to have what I got.

No one can ever know just how amazing it seems.

A strike from the Heavens and brought from the mystical glare.

Swarming through my skin and hiding in my hand.

I hold all of the magic that grace's the air.

I feel as the first girl to take the mighty stand.

I can bring the light,

I can summon with all of my will.

My amazing gift,

it brings all of the shine.

Everything amazing,

I can claim as mine.

Everything amazing,

I can claim as mine.

One day I was just sitting in my room, admiring my claws and humming my new song. Father was not even home, so I knew I was safe to show off my power to myself without getting caught. Then there was a horrified woman's scream outside. Along with it was the sound of something on fire. I pulled my claws back in and rushed out of the back door. I followed the sounds of the burning and screaming, and came to the sight of someone burning alive. The face had already been burnt away; I could not see who it was. I, along with all of the other bystanders, could do nothing but watch in horror as this poor soul gradually became nothing more than a smoldering pile of ashes.

"LEVI, NOOOO!" shouted the woman who was screaming earlier. Her name was Eartha Miller. She had been standing near the poor burning being, and now that he, or she, was nothing more than ashes, she dropped to her knees and sobbed over them. It was clear now that the ashes used to be her husband, Levi Miller.

"Mrs. Miller," said the preacher as he approached Eartha, "what hath happened to thy husband?"

"I...I...I don't know," she said, crying in between words. "I was just telling him goodbye... I was going to the market... and then he... he..." before she could say one more word, she burst out into louder, relentless crying.

"He just caught on fire, and with no explanation?" asked the preacher. All Eartha could do was shake her head up and down. Shook up and down as her eyes cascaded her poor husband's ashes with tears of sorrow and broken heart.

"WHO HATH DONE THIS?" shouted the preacher. All standing around the scene remained silent. I was just as curious. How could Levi Miller have just caught on fire? And if someone caused it, how? "I REPEAT, WHO HATH DONE THIS! DOST ANY SOUL WANT TO STEP FORWARD AND BEG FORGIVENESS?" Still not a soul moved. Not my best friend, Emily Carter, not that coated swine, Edward Hawthorne, not my father, Jonathan Fern, nor me or anyone else. Then the preacher turned his eyes to me. Did he suspect it was I? "Miss Desiree Fern," he said.

"Yes preacher?" I responded.

"Dost thou know what happened?" he asked with narrow eyes.

"I do not, preacher."

"Thy house is the closest to the Miller house," he said, still with suspicion in his voice. It was true; the Millers were the closest neighbors of father and me.

"T'was not I," I said. I tried to sound as patient as I could, even though fire hotter than the flames that killed Levi Miller were burning in my blood.

"Thou hath been a sinner for long, we all know that," everyone shook their heads in agreement. "We can believe thou doing anything." The preacher went on.

"I SAID IT WAS NOT I!" I shouted, letting the fire in my blood escape, "HOW DO WE KNOW THAT THOU HATH NOT DONE IT?" I challenged the "oh so wise and pure preacher."

"HOW DARE THEE ACUSE ME?" he roared with a voice like a thundering bear.

"It could have been thee, or maybe thy own student, EDWARD HAWTHORNE!"

"I COULD DO NO SUCH THING, SLUT!" he shouted as he walked up to me.

"Thou hath been a pretender for all of thy life, maybe thou hath done this to let out thy inner Satan!"

"I HAVE NO INNER SATAN!"

"SATAN WOULD BEAT A WOMAN!" the bystanders all gasped at my words.

"Don't make me beat thee again!"

"If thee dares to, I will beat thee back!"

"THAT IS ENOUGH!" shouted the preacher, "DESIRE AND EDWARD, STEP AWAY FROM EACHOTHER!" Edward and I sneered at each other one last time, then we turned and walked a distance from each other. "Now," the preacher went on, "this horrible tragedy is what we must concentrate on. Any feuds will just have to wait. My dear, Mrs. Miller, allow me to escort thee to the church."

"Not without my husband's ashes."

"All right, Edward and I shall help thee gather them up. And as for everyone else, look out for any signs of the Lord of Darkness! This can only be his work! We shall find out who did this no matter what!" After his words, the town's folk departed. Everyone looked at me in a suspicious way. That brought me so much anger. The preacher, Hawthorne, all of them. They all thought that I did it. Well all of those waste-minded worms were wrong. And if they were going to suspect me, then I was going to suspect them.

The rest of the day of Levi Miller's death, I found that my relationship with father was even worse. He was a well-respected man of faith. And me of course not, and being the suspect of Miller's death, caused his good reputation to fade. The town had always respected him, but I, being the way I am, had always done harm to his reputation. And being the prime suspect for the mysterious death by fire only made it worse. Father practically stopped talking to me. There was now little difference in him being home and being away. The few times he did speak to me were accusations of me knowing how the burning happened. Then I would always turn it back on him by accusing him, since he was out of the house when it happened. That always enraged him and made him want to beat me. But he remembered our last confrontation on the day before my birthday. So, he would instead beat the table. So bad was our relationship for the rest of the day; but I was used to us not living happily together, and did not let it stop me from enjoying my good times. Nor did I let the flea-skinned cowards of the town stop me.

The day following the burning of Levi Miller, I left my tension filled house to go for a swim. Everyone I passed still gave me looks of suspicion, but I would always counter it by doing it back at them. Everyone I passed was on their way to the funeral for Levi Miller. I did not know Miller personally, so I felt I had no business going. All I was concerned about was keeping my own life exciting. I looked back at the funeral, and saw that everyone was there, except for two people, Arthur Monroe, and Emily.

"That's odd," I said to myself. I hoped they were all right. I decided to check their houses just for certainty. I looked in Emily's house, but she wasn't there. My heart began to pulse; where was my only friend? I rushed to Arthur's house all of the way at the end of the town, to see if he was there, and if he knew where Emily was. The door was closed, but I could hear a scream from inside. Emily's scream. The door was locked, I couldn't open it. I tired the windows, but they were locked two. But I had to get in; I heard Emily scream some more, but now it was muffled, as if her mouth were being covered. Then I remembered my mystical claws. So, I used the one on the finger close to my thumb to cut the hinges off of the door. Then I pulled in my claw, and kicked the door down. There, I saw Arthur pinning Emily to the floor, covering her mouth, and trying to strip off her clothes. They looked at me in surprise.

"Arthur!" I shouted, "What art thou doing to my friend?"

"How did thee break down the door?" asked Arthur.

"That's no matter now; I asked what art thou doing?"

Emily managed to shake her mouth lose from his hand and say, "He was trying to rape me!"

"What?" I shouted with anger.

"I learned it from thee," Arthur said with a devilish smirk.

"HELL WASTE!" I hollered at his preposterous claim, "LEAVE MY FRIEND ALONE!"

"How about thou join in with us?" he said with lust in his eyes, "Thou hath introduced me to love-making, surely thee would love to go at it again with me, and with thy friend."

"After what thou art doing? I'd retch at the very thought!"

"Well, at least thy pretty friend will get to." The pile of rat bones said as he turned back to Emily and began to force his slobbery lips onto hers. Emily struggled helplessly, and I knew I had to help.

"GET OFF OF HER!" I shouted, as I ran after him and grabbed him by the neck, and began to squeeze. I could hear him choking, then he turned and punched me in the mouth, forcing me to release. I didn't lose any teeth, but I still began to bleed in my mouth a little. Then he tackled me to the ground. Quickly, I pulled up my right fist and punched him in his mouth. He lost three of his teeth. Then he threw his weight on top of me, pinning me to the floor. His face was close to mine; I seized this opportunity to bite him on his right cheek. He shrieked at the pain, but my teeth held their grip, nearly taking the flesh off of his cheek. Then he grabbed my neck and began to choke me. I felt all of the air emptying from my body. I couldn't last much longer. Then suddenly, my mystical claws came out of my fingers and stabbed him though the chest, right were his heart is. His blood splattered on me, then he fell limp on my body. Dead!

"AAAAAAHHHHHHH!" screamed Emily. I quickly pulled back in my claws, and in a repulsed fashion, pushed Arthur's dead, bleeding body off of me. I was taken by the biggest shock of my life. He died, just like that. I killed him. But I didn't mean to. I released my claws by accident. Emily could not take the sight off the blood. She turned around and began to retch all over the floor. I just sat there in shock, looking at the body, and the blood all over my dress. Emily finished retching, then she turned to me.

"What did thou do to him?" she asked.

"I...I...it was an accident," I said.

"But how? That was unnatural. What was it, Desiree?" I figured I had no choice but to show her. So, reluctantly, I summoned my claws from my left fingers, right in her view for her to see. Her eyes grew to an enormous width, and her mouth hung open.

"Merciful God!" she said with so much disbelief.

"I know," I said back," I've had this power since my birthday. I just woke up with it that morning. These claws destroy whatever they touch." Then I pulled them back in.

"Witch," she whispered.

"No Emily. I'm not a witch. I've never even touched a spell."

"WITCH! THOU ART A WITCH, SATAN'S DAUGHTER!"

"NO, NO! Please Emily," I said with tears falling from my eyes. "Thou art my best friend, please don't be afraid. I love thou like a sister, please don't hate me." Slowly her face changed from frightened to sympathetic. She walked over to me and helped me up, then she embraced me with much affection. I embraced her back, crying even harder. "I thank thee Emily, I think thee with gratitude."

"I love thou tooDesiree, and I want to help in any way I can."

"Well, I think the first thing we should do is get rid of the body."

"Right, let us do that." So, we both carried a side of Arthur's body, walked it out to the woods, and threw it into the James River.

"So," asked Emily, "how many people know of thy power?"

"Only thee. I've kept it a secret since I discovered it."

"And you do not know where it came from?"

"No, no knowledge at all. I woke up on the morn of my birthday and just had it. I loved it at first, but now after what it has just done, I hate it. I don't know why such a curse is happening to me."

"Maybe it's a punishment."

"From God?"

"Yes, for how thee hath behaved thy whole life."

"No, I refuse to believe that. My power just killed a man; if God is so great, would he sacrifice a man's life just to teach me a lesson?"

"Well, Arthur did become a rapist, someone who's expendable. And it was thy fault that he became one."

"WHAT?" I shouted in anger.

"It only ads more truth to my belief. By seducing him, thou hath turned a pure man to sin, someone expendable for thy punishment."

"SHUT UP!"

"But, Desiree, I really believe…"

"SHUT UP! AFTER ALL I'M GOING THROUGH THIS IS NOT WHAT I NEED RIGHT NOW!"

"But I…"

"I SAID SHUT UP! JUST LEAVE ME ALONE, TRAMP! GO AWAY AND NEVER SHOW THY FACE TO ME AGAIN!" with all of my inner rage let out, I noticed the tears filling up her eyes, and the little gasps of a baby escaping her lips. Poor Emily, I really hurt her feelings. "I…I," I tried to speak, but I couldn't help but cry two," I'm sorry Emily!" then I threw my arms around her and embraced her apologetically. "I'm so sorry! It's just that I'm scared. I don't know what's going to happen next."

"It's all right, Desiree. I'm here, I will help thee." She said as she embraced me back.

"Oh thank thee Emily, best of friends, thank thee."

Emily and I had to hide all traces of Arthur's death. So we made it back to his house and cleaned up his blood and Emily's retched up waste. The town was still at the funeral, so we still had time to get rid of our blood stained clothes. First we went back to her house, and I destroyed her dress with my claws while she put on a new one. Then I said goodbye to my friend, and went back to my house to do the same thing to my dress. After destroying it, I noticed that my mirror for my bosom pocket had blood on it. I could have just washed the blood off in water. But instead, after looking at myself in it, seeing the blood that stained my reflection, the blood of a man that I killed, I touched it with the claw on the finger next to my thumb. Destroying it forever.

The day following the funeral was terrible. When everyone noticed that Arthur Monroe was missing, his door was broken down, and that Emily and I were the only ones to not attend the funeral, we were both suspects now. Suspects of the burning of Levi Miller, and the disappearance of Arthur Monroe. The whole day, Emily and I were treated to suspicious eyes. It was awful. I didn't mind being a suspect; I was used to being an outcast. But poor Emily, she could not deal with it, she had not the strength. It was all because of my horrible claws. They did this to me and my friend. They ruined our lives. To express my anger, I wrote a new song about them on the second day following the funeral.

<u>My Life Kills</u>

Thou hath betrayed me,

thou hath slayed me,

thou hath become a flaming

traitor!

I once loved thee,

now I want to shove thee,

thou art my biggest

hater!

Why hath thou come?

Why hath thou deceived?

Why hath thou betrayed

me?

If thou hates me,

if thou feels detestful,

then why won't thou let me

be?

My life kills,

kills with spite,

just like thee does,

every night!

I hate thee so,

hate with all my might,

I only wish I could put

thee right!

My life kills,

kills with spite,

just like thee does,

every night!

I hate thee so,

hate with all my might,

I only wish I could put

thee right!

Go away from me,

don't ever let me see,

thy hideous glowing

sight!

Thy man killing strike,

bringing life to the night,

what I never wanted in my

life!

I don't feel the same,

I don't feel relieved,

feel like a dyeing

tree!

The worst I can be,

so hurt and resentful,

and it's all because of

thee!

My life kills,

kills with spite,

just like thee does,

every night!

I hate thee so,

hate with all my might,

I only wish I could put

thee right!

My life kills,

kills with spite,

just like thee does,

every night!

I hate thee so,

hate with all my might,

I only wish I could put

thee right!

The following day, a scream was heard across town. Father and I rushed from our house to where the scream came from; the Depp's house, just 50 feet from ours. The entire town gathered around it, and witnessed the Depp parents crying over the smoldering ashes of their six year old son, Benjamin. It was another mysterious burning. Just like the last one, there was no sign of how it happened. The preacher stepped forward.

"THIS HATH GONE FAR ENOUGH! COME TOMORROW, THERE WILL BE A HANGING! IT WILL BE OUR TWO SUSPECTS, EMILY CARTER AND DESIREE FERN!"

"NO!" shouted Emily, "I DID NOT DO IT!"

"NOR DID I!" I shouted, "THERE ART NO SMOKE ON OUR SOULS!"

"THERE HATH BEEN SMOKE ON THY SOULS SINCE THE FIRST BURNING! YEE TWO SHALL HANG IN THE MORN! PUNISHMENT FOR DISTURBING OUR PURIST OF LIVING!"

After the meeting that called for the death my friend and I, I wanted to talk to Emily. I was hoping on us comforting each other. But, Emily was too filed with sorrow and dread, she did not want to talk to me, nor anyone. She just wanted to be left alone, until our day of reckoning. Leaving me to do the same. Leaving me with no one to talk to, no one to turn to for comfort. All I could do was wait, wait for that hungry noose to grasp my life into its hands.

That night, as I slept in my room for the last time, I felt a hand shaking my right shoulder; someone was trying to wake me. I opened my eyes; it was still the middle of the night. It was dark, but thanks to the bright full moon, I could see clearly who my disturber was. It was Edward Hawthorne.

"Hawthorne?" I said quietly, "What art thou doing in my room?"

"I came through thy window."

"What?"

"I'm sorry I did that, but I had to talk with thee."

"With me? Why would thou want to talk with me? I'm just a sinful, wicked, witch-slut."

"I don't believe thou art a witch," he said with much honesty and seriousness in his voice.

"Thou does not?" I asked.

"No. Thou may love to act sinful, but thou art not a monster, or one who practices witchcraft."

"How can you be so sure?"

"I've observed thee from a far for so long. Observed how free and fun loving thou art, but never seen any sign of evil. When I look at thee, I do not see a witch, all I see, is a beautiful lantern."

Is this the real Edward Hawthorne? I asked myself. Why was he praising me so much, and making me feel heat for him once more?

"I... I thought thou hated me," I said.

"I've never hated thee. Thy energy, thy loving of life, thy brave behavior and brave expressions of thyself. I have never seen a soul so free and so unafraid to show it. I've admired that for so long. No one else here would dare do what thee does."

"Then why did thou hit me?" Edward just looked down at the floor, and did not say a word. "Well?" I asked.

"Pressure," he said.

"Pressure?" I repeated.

"The pressure from our town. The pressure of being told to hate sin, being raised to be a preacher for God, being expected of purity and virtue all of the time by all around me," the longer he talked, tears began to emerge from his eyes, "Then thee came onto me that day. I felt excitement, a feeling I never knew was real, but knowing it was wrong, feeling the weight of what I had been taught, and how everyone wants me to be. Then, my frustration just lashed out beyond my control. And I'm so sorry Desiree." He dropped to his knees, his head on the side of my bed as he wept like a frightened child. "I implore thy forgiveness, Desiree. Please forgive me. I love thee." I again asked myself, *Is this real Edward Hawthorne?*

"Love?" I asked.

"Yes, I've loved thee for some time, and now I'm so sure of it. I had to let thee know before the hanging. I beg thee to forgive me for the way I was." He kept his face on my bed, continuing to weep. I could suddenly feel my heart pound unbearably hard. I raised my left hand to touch him, but quickly I pulled it back. I did not want my wretched claws to come out and kill him. So, I kept my left hand back, and touched his head with my right hand.

"I forgive thee," I said. He stopped crying, and raised his head up to look his beautiful eyes into mine. I put my hand under his chin, holding it in my palm. "I never realized how much strain thee hath been under for so long. And I'm so sorry to. I would never want thee to feel torn and tortured."

"Oh my love, thou art so good to me. I know thou art not a witch."

"Well, actually, I do have a strange secret." Part of me said that I should not reveal to him my dark gift, but I knew I could trust him. I knew I could tell him.

"A secret?"

"I can't set people on fire, but I do have a strange power."

"What is it?"

Then, hesitantly, I showed him my claws. They emerged from my left fingers, illuminating the dark room. Edward just starred at them, his eyes wide, and his mouth looking as if it was going to drop from his face. "Does this terrify thee?" I asked with a look of sympathy in my eyes.

"No. It's amazing. A true gift from God." My heart instantly picked up even greater speed. I pulled my claws back in, and began to stroke his right cheek with my left fingers, gently and soothingly. His eyes were closed with bliss and tranquility. Then I leaned forward, and kissed him on the lips passionately. Our kiss began to carry on, and he crawled into bed with me, we wrapped our arms around each other, our lips never parting, and we made sweet, passionate love. Myself, and my hope delivering savior.

Dawn was approaching by the time our love making ended. Edward was looking immensely happy, and so was I. Love making had never been this enjoyable and full of pleasure for me before. I felt like I was falling forever. And I loved it.

"Desiree, my love." said Edward.

"Yes," I responded in an airy voice, thanks the emotional pounding of my heart.

"I will not let them hang thee, or thy friend." He started to get out of the bed to go back to the window. "Just let the guards bring thee to the hanging as the town expects. I will step up and tell the preacher what I know about thee within my very soul. I will tell him that he's wrong, and so is the town. You and Emily are innocent maidens, who do not carry flames in their souls."

"Oh sweet Edward," I said in my airy voice, unable to escape the smile on my face, "thou art the most virtuous human being." Then Edward walked over to my sprawled out body, and then he bent down and kissed my forehead.

"I love my Desiree," he said.

"And I love Edward," I responded, nearly fainting.

I allowed the guards to bring myself and Emily up to the hanging stage, just as Edward advised. I was barely awake, still exhausted from that passionate night. I would have probably not even been able to fight of the guards if I wanted to. We were standing on our barrels, the nooses being fastened around our necks. Then the preacher stood in front of us, facing the audience to give a speech.

"THESE TWO, EMILY CARTER AND DESIREE FERN, ARE FOUND GUILTY FOR THE CRIME OF MURDER AND WITCHCRAFT! THEY SHALL HANG BY THE NECK UNTIL THEY ARE DEAD, AND MY THE LORD HAVE MERCY ON THEIR SOULS!"

"STOP!" shouted my sweetest Edward from the crowd.

"Young Hawthorne," said the preacher to his apprentice and adopted son, "what be the meaning of this?" Edward stormed up the steps onto the stage and confronted the preacher.

"These young ladies are innocent!"

"What? All signs of the deaths by fire, and the disappearance of Arthur Monroe point to them. We must do what must be done. FOR OUR GOOD LORD'S SAKE!" the crowd cheered at that, even my own father.

"I love Desiree Fern, and I know she would not commit these acts!"

"THOU LOVES WHO?" shouted the angered preacher.

"I love Desiree Fern!" Edward repeated, "I always have!"

"THOU LOVES A SLUT?"

"I don't care what you call her! I love my darling Desiree! And if Emily Carter is her friend, then she is mine two!" Emily's ominous eyes began to look happy at my love's brave words. "I know in my heart that these two hath not done these crimes!"

"NO, BUT I HAVE!" shouted a voice from the crowd. We all moved our eyes to the speaker. I could not believe who spoke those words.

Part 3

It was father!

"Mr. Fern, what art thou saying?" asked the preacher. Father replied in a frightening way. He blasted strings of fire from his fingers on both hands, turning the preacher to ashes, just like Levi Miller, and Benjamin Depp. The town screamed and fled to their houses. Men were pulling their wives, wives were pulling their children, everyone retreated to the safety of their homes. The only ones left staring in awe and fright were Edward, Emily and I. Quickly I used my claws to cut the nooses that were holding back Emily and me.

"FATHR!" I shouted, "HOW DOST THOU DO THAT?"

"A gift," he said, "a gift from the Devil. Just like thy mysterious claws."

"The Devil?" I asked.

"Yes," then he worked his way upon the stage to speak to me face to face. Emily and Edward were watching from the side. "It all began when youwere born," father went along, "and when thy mother died in childbirth." He then began his long, dark story.

"Thy mother and I were very much in love. In love with each other, and in love with the Lord. No one believed more than us in faith, Puritanism, and God. Our love for God and for each other was what drove us to live happily, and appreciate the beauty of the world.

"But then, came her day of labor. She was giving birth to thee, Desiree. And as she did it, she began to slip away. She fought hard; I kneeled by her side, grasping her hand, and praying to the Holy father harder than I have ever prayed in my life. With her very last breath, she pushed thee out. I was deliriously happy when the doctor handed thou to me, and said that thee was going to make it. But my beautiful, loving wife was gone. This was the Lord's way of showing His gratitude for me! After living a sinless life, praising Him, loving Him and worshipping Him all of my life; he took away the only woman I ever loved! From that very moment, I hated God! I hated

Him, and all to do with Him! Of course, I never told a soul about my honest feelings to keep myself out of trouble in this strictly religious society. But for the first two weeks of thy life, I held in my passionate hatred for the Holy Father.

"Then one night, as I was sleeping, you in thy baby basket safely near me, Satan himself appeared at the left of my bed. He woke me up, glaring down at me with his soulless, black eyes. I was terrified at first, and I rushed over to thou to protect you. But he did not try to hurt us. Instead, he made me an offer. Knowing how deeply I hated God, he offered me a chance to get revenge on Him. He said he would give me the power to shoot strings Hellfire out of my fingers, and with it, destroy all of the people in the world who believe in God; starting with this town. With my relentless hatred, and my thirst for revenge on God for taking my true love away from me, I said yes. But only if he would give my precious daughter a power two. Give her a power so she could help me carry out that noble deed, so me and my beloved child could rule the world together, after destroying all who carry faith in their pockets.

"The generous Lord of Darkness agreed. He said that I would have my power once he left to return to Hell, and that once thou hath reached thy sixteenth birthday, thee will have the power to make deadly claws emerge from thy own left fingers. He kept his word. Once he left, I could summon flames of Hell from my fingers, and I knew that sixteen years from now, thee would wield thy deadly power as well.

"But, until thou hath received thy gift, I had to prepare thee. I had to make thee hate God as much as I. I had to be as abusive towards thee as possible, and fill thy mind with the truth of how punishing and terrifying God is, so thou would develop hatred toward Him. Along with that, I had to continue wearing my mask of a loving devoted puritan, so devoted that I'm deemed worthy of training apprentices, like young Hawthorne here. Carry on a lie for sixteen years.

"Then, when thou hath finally received thy gift on thy sixteenth birthday, (as thou did, I can see) I had to give thee a week to get used to it and learn how to control it. Then, I had to start killing people in secret, and allow all signs to point to thee, until the town would finally decide to hang thee; the pivotal moment for thee. I knew that by that time, thee would finally be hungering for the blood of all believers for the way they have always treated thee.

"Now, it's finally happened my dear," father said as he moved in and embraced me. He never embraced me until now. I felt so touched that I wanted to cry. But I knew I had to keep my attention on this terrible situation. Father expected me to help him destroy every one, something I could not bear to do. "Now Desiree, dost thou understand why I had always been so cruel to thee?"

"Yes father, I do."

"Well that's in the past. I can make up for it and be the loving father thou hath always wanted. But first, we must carry out Satan's plan. Then the two of us shall roam the world, doing whatever we want, and live the happiest life a father and daughter would ever want." Then he turned to Emily and Edward, my two dearest friends. "Now it's time to kill all believers in that flaming God, starting with these two!" He raised his left hand and prepared to fire at them.

"NOOOO!" I screamed as I pushed his arm away, causing him to shoot at the air, and knocking him off of the stage. "RUN EMILY, RUN EDWARD, RUN!" Emily shook her head up and down and ran to her home, but Edward stayed rooted to his spot. "EDWARD!"

"NO DESIREE, I'M NOT LEAVING THEE!"

"DESIREE!" shouted father from the ground. "WHY ART THOU BEING FOOLISH? AFTER THE WAY THIS TOWN HATH TREATED THEE? DOST THOU WANT TO CARRY OUT SATAN'S PLAN?"

"No father! This is not right! These people do not deserve to die!"

"YES THEY DO, THOU IDOT! PRAISING THAT LYING, UNCARING GOD, PRETEDNING THEY LOVE TO WORSHIP HIM, WHEN REALLY THEY ALL WANT TO TURN TO THE DEVIL SOMEWHERE DEEP DOWN INSIDE!"

"I'm not like thou father! I've already killed Arthur Monroe, and I still feel terrible about it!"

"What?" shouted Edward.

"Thou hath killed Monroe?" father asked excitedly.

"Yes!" I answered, "But it was an accident! I had no intention of what I did. And I have no intention of killing anyone in this town, or the world, who believe in God! Especially my best friend, Emily, or my love, Edward Hawthorne!" After those last words, Edward and I briefly gazed into each other's eyes. Then I jumped down to help up my father. "Please father, mother would not want us to do the Devil's work. Please understand my words father." I pleaded to him, but he did not seem to acknowledge any thing I said. His hatred and rage was blocking out my plead. He tried to hit me, but again I grabbed his arm, stopping his attack. But then he kicked me, sending me sprawling backwards and on to the ground.

"AFTER ALL I'VE DONE FOR THEE, THIS IS HOW THOU ART SHOWS GRADITUDE! AFTER GIVING THEE A GREAT POWER AND A PROMISE FOR A LIFE OF EVENTUAL PEACE! DESIREE MY DAUGHTER, THOU ART AS UNGRATEFUL AS GOD!" Father then blasted fire at me; quickly I extended my claws and slashed it away.

"Please father, we don't have to fight," I pleaded. He did not listen, he only shot at me again, and again I slashed it away, still lying on the ground. Out of the corner of my eye, I saw Edward quickly grab my noose, run up to father, and try to strangle him from behind. It looked like he had him; father struggled and looked as if he were choking miserably. But father quickly elbowed Edward in the face with a painful force. My love lost his grip, and then father struck with his fist sending him slamming to the ground unconscious. Father tore off the noose and prepared to set fire to Edward. My love was about to die, this brought forth my rage, now I was ready to fight my father. I charged at him with my claws ready to strike, shouting, "NOOOOO!" But father jumped away, causing my slash to narrowly miss him. He fired again, but I slashed the flames away. We glared at each other intensely, my claws extended, and his fingers ready to blast again. He fired at me, but I slashed it away, then I charged in closer. Every time I got in close he managed to avoid my attack. I had to keep our distance short. That would give me the advantage, while a long distance would favor him. He once again dodged me, and this time he got far enough to shoot at me. I didn't have time to slash again, so this time I jumped to my right. I felt the heat nip at my legs, but there was no burn. At that second, I noticed a pitchfork on the ground, quickly I picked it up and threw it at him. He tried to dodge, but his right arm got cut and he hollered in pain. I took advantage of his moment of vulnerability to charge in and give him a fatal slash. But quickly, he tripped me with his right foot, sending me sliding on my stomach to the ground. Before I could get back up, father stood on top of my arms. With his enormous weight suffocating the blood in my arms, and all of my weariness from our battle, I could not get up. I expected him to kill me at that very moment, but instead, he started talking.

"Desiree, my beloved child, I am so sorry," he sounded sad, deeply and sincerely sad. I turned my head to the left to look from the corner of my left eye. His eyes were clouding with tears. "I did not want for this to happen. I love thee, and I only want what's best for thee, so that is why I must finish you off. But just remember, when thee makes it to Heaven, unlike me, that I love thee. I always have, and I'm so sorry that I have to do this." I could feel tears in my eyes. He never spoke to me in such a loving, caring way before. But then he raised his arms, ready to set me to the Devil's flames. Quickly thinking, I extended my claws and slashed through the ground, creating a large gap underneath my left arm, causing father to lose his balance and fall to the right. He was down, and with all of the swiftness I could muster, jumped over top of him, raised my claws, and with tear-filled eyes, stabbed him through the chest, and worked my claws up through his head. Now all I was left staring at was the blood and remaining body parts of my only father, whom I had always loved.

Before I could mourn any longer, the villagers suddenly came out of their houses, making angry cries and carrying pitchforks. Edward finally woke up and ran to my side.

"WITCH, WITCH, WITCH!" cried the town.

"HAVE ALL OF THEE GONE MAD?" shouted Edward, "DESIREE HATH SAVED US!"

"THAT GIRL POSSESSES POWERS FROM THE DEVIL!" shouted a man from the crowd.

"SHE DOST NOT BELONG HERE!" shouted a woman.

"EITHER SHE LEAVES, OR SHE DIES!" another man shouted. The whole village hollered in agreement, raising their pitchforks to the sky.

"UNGRATEFUL DEMONS!" shouted Edward with all of the strength in his voice, "SHE HATH SAVED US ALL!"

"LOVER OF THE WITCH!" shouted another villager, "HE SHALL DIE TWO!" The village shouted with agreement to that as well.

"NO!" I shouted, "EDWARD AND I HAVE DONE NO WRONG! EMILY PLEASE!" I said to Emily when I noticed her in the crowd, looking scarred and confused, "Please my friend speak for us. You know I'm not a witch."

Emily looked even more confused and scarred. Her eyes looked to me, then to the crowd, then back to me. She obviously did not know what to do. Then her eyes began to tear up, and she turned to me and shouted, "DECEIVING WITCH!"

"WHAT?" I shouted, not believing the words coming from my best friend.

"THOU ART A WITCH, THOU HATH MANIPULATED ME INTO BEING THY FRIEND!"

"THAT'S NOT TRUE EMILY, YOU KNOW THAT!"

"THOU BETRAYER!" Edward shouted to her.

"SHE HATH MANIPULATED ME!" Emily shouted to the village, "SHE IS A SATANIC SERPENT, A WITCH!" The audience agreed once again. Emily looked at me with eyes filled with tears, clearly looking for sympathy, even though she knew she was betraying me. Well, that coward was not going to get it. I felt my teeth gritting, and my eyes squinting in rage. She was not going to get my sympathy, no one was! In fact, they were all not going to live!

I flashed my claws, raised them in front of the crowd, and hollered, "ALL RIGHT THEN, IF THEE ALL WANTS AN EVIL WITCH, THEN THEE ALL WILL GET ONE!" I charged at the closest person, and stabbed him through the chest, and then I angrily ripped out my claws and slashed off the head of a nearby woman. The town dropped their pitchforks, screamed in terror, and fled before me. But they could not escape; no one could escape my claws. At every turn, I found a new pathetic victim. Body after body, the pathetic swine went down. Blood coloring the ground and the houses, body parts scattered about, my delicious revenge was coming full force. Oh the ecstasy and epiphany that lifted my spirits, oh the inner devil I finally let out. Now all were dead, except for that ex-best friend of mine, Emily. She stood frozen like a tree.

"Please, have forgiveness Desiree, please let me live!" the cowardly traitor pleaded.

"THOU UGLY, STUPID, COWARDLY FLEA! THIS IS WHAT THOU HATH DESERVED FOR SO LONG!" I ran at her with the brute force speed of a pack of wolves, and slashed her entire body in half. "SEE THEE IN HELL, CARTER! SEE THEE IN HELL!"

Once I noticed the tears in Emily's eyes, after she joined in with the town against me and Edward, that killing spree was what I fantasized. But that was not what happened. Though that was what I felt I desperately wanted to do, I admit that. But I could not bring myself to father's level. So instead, I grabbed Edward by the hand, and we fled from the town. Fled from the townspeople who so badly wanted us dead. We ran and ran, until we escaped the townspeople before they could kill us. We were safe in a small, tranquil, secluded forest. A peaceful place to escape to, but Edward was not feeling so peaceful.

"Those betrayers! Desiree, thou should have killed them! They deserve it! After saving them from thy Hell-spawned father, they tried to kill thee! Let's go back, so thee can teach them a lesson."

"No dearest Edward, I cannot."

"Why?"

"I'd be doing exactly what father wanted. I'd be just like him, and I cannot do that. Though I am relentlessly angry at them, especially Emily, whom I thought was my best friend. But, they do not deserve it."

"How could they not deserve it?"

"They are not evil. They are just confused. Their minds are consumed by their fear-stricken beliefs. But people change. Perhaps someday, they will realize that their mad beliefs are wrong. And I still care for them, especially Emily, the one I have so many fond friendship memories of."

"Oh Desiree, my darling," said to me my loving Edward, as he wrapped his arms around me, holding me like an angel holding a harp, "Why could not the townspeople be like thee? Why cannot all people be like thee?"

After his kind words, I broke into tears. I went to my knees, laid my arms on the ground, and sobbed miserably into my arms.

"Desiree, what's the matter?" Edward asked.

"My father, I killed him."

"I know. Thou hath done the right thing."

"I know that, but he was my father. I loved him, and still do. Why did I have to do it? Why?" I felt so miserable. The most I've ever felt. Edward began to comfort me by rubbing my back.

"It's all right love, I understand," he said, "it must have been awful for thee. I'm sorry." I then got back up to my knees, and wiped the tears from my eyes.

"I have to pray," I said.

"Pray?" he repeated in amazement, "but I thought thou never prays."

"That's because, up until now, I had no motivation for it."

"What's it for?"

"Please Edward, its private. I prefer not to discuss it."

"Oh I'm sorry, I won't ask again."

"Thank thee."

And so I began my first prayer in years. I put my hands together, closed my eyes, bowed my head, and said in my thoughts, "Oh Holy God, please forgive my father. I pray to thee for him to be forgiven.

I know he hath done great evil, but he is my father, and I love him with all of my heart. Please have mercy on him. Please give him your grace, your understanding, and your forgiveness. I pray to thee, for my father. Let us meet in Thy land when I die, Thy holy land. Where we can finally live peacefully together. Together for all eternity, and with Thy light pouring through us, and onto this dark world, so our love can bring it some of thy light, for all eternity.

AMEN"

I wiped the heartfelt tears from my eyes after my prayer, and then got back to my feet, and Edward and I continued walking. We made it to the sea. Naturally, we knew what we had to do. We had to sail off into the sea, and find a new home. A home that would accept us. A home where we could be free.

Using my claws, I easily cut down several trees, and Edward and I made them into a small ship, just big enough for two. We set sail once it was complete. As we sailed off, I looked out into the beautiful ocean, my love standing behind with his passionate arms around me. I felt free again. Looking out into the beautiful ocean, and sailing ever so smoothly, with my love holding me in his embrace, I just had to let out a song.

We Have the Strength

My love and I,

hath set off and begun to fly,

freedom to seek,

that we will,

seek for it, through heat and chill.

We will witness it all,

the beauty that comes to call,

of this world,

that may be dark,

but even though, we'll leave our mark.

We still have it,

the strength we bring,

to let our souls and spirits ring,

just like all,

in this world so tall,

we have the strength,

and power I sing.

On the sea we ride,

beauty on every side,

I feel the joy,

and love for life,

I always had for days and night.

The poetry of the sea,

that shines in front of me,

and to guide us two,

light us the way,

lead us on, until that day.

We still have it,

the strength we bring,

to let our souls and spirits ring,

just like all,

in this world so tall,

we have the strength,

and power I sing.

Just like all,

in this world so tall,

we have the strength,

and power I sing.

we have the strength,

and power I sing.

THE END

About the Author

Zachary Duresky is a college graduate from Randolph Macon College in Ashland, Virginia. He graduated with a bachelor's degree in English. He began writing in high school, where he mainly did poetry. In college he moved on to short stories and then eventually his first novel, "Desiree Fern." "Desiree Fern" is a personal accomplishment for Zachary Duresky. She is his favorite creation. She has always served as a symbol of comfort for him whenever he felt down. To him, she represents being who you are and not letting those around you control you. Zachary Duresky lives in Glen Allen, Virginia, where he enjoys the simple pleasures of films, television, books, good food, and writing of course. He comes from a loving family that has always been there to support him and love him. He has had to struggle through many aspects of life because he was diagnosed with Asperger's syndrome when he was six. But like Desiree, he made it through life his own way and made the best out of all life had to offer.